When the king and queen hold a party to celebrate the birth of their daughter, Aurora, everyone is invited. Or almost *everyone – they forget to ask the wicked fairy Maleficent! She goes to the party anyway, just to cast a spell – a really evil one – on the little princess. But luckily Aurora's three fairy godmothers Flora, Fauna, and Merryweather are there to help...*

British Library Cataloguing in Publication Data
Disney, Walt
Walt Disney's Sleeping Beauty.—(Disney Stories)
I. Series
823'.914[J] PZ7
ISBN 0-7214-1024-3

First edition

Printed in England

Walt Disney's

Sleeping Beauty

Ladybird Books

There once lived a king and queen who held a great feast to celebrate the birth of their baby daughter, Aurora. One of the guests at the feast was the king of a nearby country, and he had a young son called Philip.

During the feast, the two kings made plans for Prince Philip and Princess Aurora to marry as soon as the princess reached her sixteenth birthday.

Princess Aurora had three fairy godmothers – Flora, Fauna, and Merryweather. Each of them came to the king's feast, bringing a special gift for the little princess.

Flora waved her hand over the cradle and said to the baby, "I give you the gift of beauty!"

Fauna smiled at the child and said, “I give you the gift of song!”

Then Merryweather fluttered over to the baby’s cradle. She raised her wand…

Suddenly there was a crack of thunder, and in stormed the wicked fairy, Maleficent. No one had invited her to the feast, and she was furious.

She glared at the baby princess lying in the cradle. "*I* have a gift for you!" she hissed.

“Before the sun sets on your sixteenth birthday,” said Maleficent, “you will prick your finger on the spindle of a spinning wheel!” She gave a mocking laugh and stroked her pet raven.

“Do you understand me?” she screeched at the king and queen. “Aurora will die!”

Maleficent swept her cloak about her face and disappeared in a cloud of purple smoke, leaving the king and queen too frightened to move.

Then Merryweather gave a gentle cough. "I, too, have a gift for Aurora," she reminded them.

Turning to the baby, Merryweather murmured, "My gift to you is *life*! When the spindle pricks your finger, you will not die. Instead, you will fall into an enchanted sleep. Only a kiss from your true love will waken you."

The king and queen decided that the princess would be safer if she moved away from the palace. So they asked the three fairy godmothers to look after her.

Flora, Fauna, and Merryweather took the princess to a little cottage in the woods. They put away their wands and pretended to be old peasant women. They didn't use the princess's real name. Instead they called her Briar Rose.

The years passed and, at last, Briar Rose's sixteenth birthday came. The three fairy godmothers wanted to make some surprise birthday presents so they sent Briar Rose out into the woods to pick berries for a pie.

Briar Rose went off happily and, after gathering the berries, she rested in a woodland glade and began to sing. Her voice floated through the trees.

That day the handsome young Prince Philip was riding through the woods on his horse, Samson. He heard Briar Rose's song and was so enchanted that he left Samson in a clearing and went on foot to find the singer.

As soon as the prince saw Briar Rose, he knew that he would always love her. She was more beautiful than anyone he had ever seen.

Meanwhile, the fairy godmothers were in a terrible muddle. Flora had decided to make a fine dress, but she had cut the material all the wrong shape and size. "This will never fit Briar Rose!" she wept.

Fauna had decided to bake a cake, but she had put in too much flour and now the cake mixture bubbled out of the bowl, all over the table. "Briar Rose will never be able to eat this!" she wailed.

"It's no use," said Merryweather. "We need to use magic if we are to get this right. I'll fetch the magic wands."

The fairy godmothers didn't know that Maleficent's black raven was perched high on their chimney pot. He was listening to every word they said.

His black eyes glittered when he heard about the magic wands. "Now how is it that three old peasant women have magic wands?" he said to himself.

Maleficent had sent the raven to search the country for Aurora. And now he was sure that he had found her fairy godmothers!

He gave a little crow of triumph.

When Briar Rose returned with her basket of berries, the presents were all ready. She loved her new dress, and the cake was delicious. But her head was full of thoughts about the stranger she had met in the woods.

Soon she began to tell her godmothers all about him. Flora and Fauna looked anxiously at Merryweather. "It's time we told Briar Rose the truth!" she said. The raven smiled as he listened.

So Briar Rose learned that she was really a princess, and that soon she would have to marry Prince Philip, the son of her father's friend.

"Today you must return to the palace, and never see this stranger again," said Merryweather.

Briar Rose was heartbroken. She didn't want to be a princess, and she didn't want to marry a prince. She had fallen in love with the handsome stranger.

The raven had heard enough. Away he flapped to tell his mistress that the search for Princess Aurora was over.

When Maleficent heard the news, she made her way to the palace. Disguised as an old woman, she hid in the shadows and watched as Aurora and her godmothers arrived at the palace. The king and queen were overjoyed to see their daughter again.

Maleficent waited for her chance. When Aurora was alone, she tricked the princess into exploring a long forgotten attic room where an old spinning wheel stood.

"Try to work it!" said Maleficent. "It's very easy." Aurora sat down at the wheel.

Instantly she pricked her finger on the spindle and fell into a deep sleep.

Maleficent disappeared, leaving only the echo of her laugh.

When the fairy godmothers discovered Aurora lying by the spinning wheel, they cast a sleeping spell over everyone in the palace.

"Now no one will ever know what has happened to our lovely princess," said Merryweather.

“Unless she is wakened by her true love’s kiss!” said Flora and Fauna.

And they suddenly remembered the handsome young stranger from the woods. “We must find him at once!” said Merryweather.

The next day, Prince Philip rode to the cottage in the woods, hoping to see Briar Rose again. But Maleficent was waiting for him. The raven had told her all about the young man who had fallen in love with Briar Rose.

Maleficent put the prince under a spell and took him back to her castle, where she threw him into her deepest dungeon. She fastened him to the wall with heavy chains and left him there.

The fairy godmothers searched everywhere for the stranger. They had discovered that he was really Prince Philip and they knew that he alone could break Maleficent's wicked spell.

They found their way to Maleficent's castle and the dungeons. Quickly they used their magic to set the prince free. They told him about Briar Rose and gave him a magic sword and shield. Prince Philip galloped off to rescue the princess.

When Maleficent discovered that the prince was free she roared with anger.

As the prince came nearer to the palace he found himself surrounded by a forest of thorns. "This is Maleficent's work!" he cried, cutting his way through with his magic sword.

When he reached the other side, a terrible black dragon stood in his path. The dragon blew hot flames and laughed. "Maleficent!" said the prince. "So it's *you*." He held up his magic shield and the dragon's scorching flames did not touch him.

The dragon soared into the air and swooped down towards the prince. The prince hurled his magic sword at the beast. The dragon was dead.

Inside the palace, Prince Philip quickly found the room where the sleeping beauty lay. "Princess Aurora!" he whispered. "My Briar Rose!"

Then he gently kissed the princess and her eyes opened. The spell was broken!

All round the palace people began to wake up from their deep sleep. Soon everyone had learned how Prince Philip had saved the princess.

And so Philip and Aurora were married. The royal wedding celebrations lasted for several days, ending with a magnificent ball. The prince and princess danced and danced all night.

No one saw the fairy godmothers sitting up in one of the chandeliers, chattering and whispering happily, watching over Princess Aurora and her prince.